Simon James is an award-winning author and illustrator of books for children
and is a regular speaker in schools and at festivals across the UK and the US.
His books include *Nurse Clementine, George Flies South, Dear Greenpeace, Leon and Bob,
Sally and the Limpet, The Day Jake Vacuumed* and the bestselling Baby Brains series.
Simon likes to draw with a dip pen and uses watercolour
paints for his illustrations. To find out more about
Simon James and his books, visit
www.simonjamesbooks.com

First published 2014 by Walker Books Ltd
87 Vauxhall Walk, London SE11 5HJ
This edition published 2015
2 4 6 8 10 9 7 5 3 1
© 2014 Simon James

The right of Simon James to be identified as author/illustrator of this work has been asserted
by him in accordance with the Copyright, Designs and Patents Act 1988

This book has been typeset in Poliphilus
Printed in China

British Library Cataloguing in Publication Data:
a catalogue record for this book is available from the British Library

ISBN 978-1-4063-6053-0

www.walker.co.uk

SIMON JAMES

REX

WALKER BOOKS
AND SUBSIDIARIES
LONDON · BOSTON · SYDNEY · AUCKLAND

Once upon about 100 million years ago, there lived a terrifying tyrannosaurus. He could crush boulders with his bare claws, he could pull whole trees out of the ground.

He scared the stegosaurus, he scared the brontosaurus,
he scared every saurus he saw!

Each night, he would stomp up into the
hills looking for an empty cave to sleep in.

The big dinosaur always slept well.
No one dared wake him.

One night, an abandoned egg
in the corner of a quiet cave
began to crack …

and slowly open.

A little dinosaur
stepped out.

It crawled and
stumbled …

and stumbled and
crawled towards a …

huge warm foot.
The little dinosaur
spoke his first words.
"Dadda!" it said.

"Who dares wake me up?" roared the big dinosaur.
"I am Tyrannosaurus Rex!"

"Rex?" repeated the little dinosaur.

"You're no Rex!" roared the big dinosaur as he stomped
off down the hill.
"I am! Wait for me, Dad," said the little dinosaur.

Rex hurried behind the big dinosaur as he
scared the diplodocus and the trigonosaurus and

terrified the triceratops, the iguanodon
and the spiky ankylosaurus.

At the end of the day, Rex followed the big dinosaur
up the hill to find a cave for the night.

"You're terrific, Dad!" said Rex.
"Will you teach me to roar like you?"

"Shhh!" grunted the big dinosaur.

"I'm trying to get to sleep."

"Good night, Dad!" whispered Rex.

"Grrrr," grumbled the big dinosaur. "Good night."

Day after day, Rex followed the big dinosaur everywhere.
When the big dinosaur roared, Rex roared.

When the big dinosaur smashed up boulders,
Rex smashed up boulders!

Before long, Rex had learned how to uproot small trees!
"You're a fast learner, Rex!" laughed the big dinosaur.

One day, the big dinosaur and Rex were relaxing by a warm river of molten lava.

"Dad?" said Rex. "When I grow up, will I be as terrifying as you? Will I, Dad?"

The big dinosaur was quiet for a moment.

"Listen, Rex," he said. "You know, I'm not
really your dad. You found me in a cave."
"Oh…" said Rex. "Really?"
"Really," said the big dinosaur.

That night, Rex couldn't sleep. He kept thinking about what the big dinosaur had said.

He wondered where he really belonged.

He decided he'd have to find out for himself.

Rex wasn't sure where to look. He hadn't
gone far when he heard a noise behind him.

Rex turned. A group of hungry eyes was staring
right back at him.

He took a big breath and roared his loudest, most fearsome roar …

and then he ran!

As fast as he could.

Through the night, Rex ran. He ran over boulders,

through swamps, over fallen trees ...

and only stopped when he was sure no one was following him.
Lonely and afraid, Rex finally fell asleep.

The next morning, Rex woke with a start.
All around, the ground was quaking.
The whole jungle shuddered
with a deafening roar.
It was the most horrible sound
Rex had ever heard.
He covered his ears.

Suddenly, a huge foot crashed down right beside him.
Rex couldn't look. He feared the worst. "Help!" he cried.

"Is that you, Rex?" said the big dinosaur.
"DAD!" shouted Rex.

"I've been looking for you everywhere!"
said the big dinosaur.

"I'm so glad it's you, Dad!" said Rex.
"You really are so scary."

The big dinosaur roared with delight. He roared so loudly, it struck fear in every dinosaur across the valley – except that is, for Rex.

"I hope I'm as terrifying as you when I grow up, Dad,"
said Rex.

"I'll make sure of it!" said the big dinosaur.
"That's what dads are for!"

Simon James

Simon James is an award-winning author and illustrator of books for children – creator of the much-loved character Baby Brains and of touching tales exploring a child's unique relationship with nature.

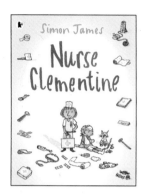

ISBN 978-1-4063-5251-1

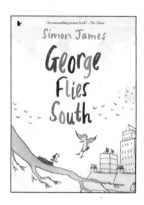

ISBN 978-1-4063-3842-3

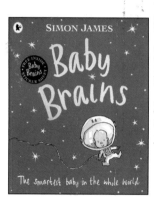

ISBN 978-1-8442-8522-8

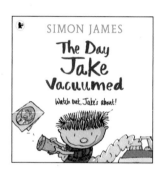

ISBN 978-1-4063-4103-4

ISBN 978-1-4063-0846-4

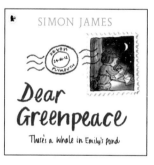

ISBN 978-1-4063-0848-8

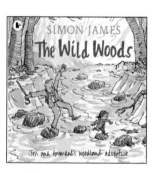

ISBN 978-1-4063-0845-7

ISBN 978-1-4063-0849-5

"Drawing always opens up a very private and delightful world. It's easy to forget that drawing in itself is a kind of magic. Drawing is good for you!" Simon James

Available from all good booksellers

www.walker.co.uk